Sophie's Dance Class

Sophie's Dance Class

Angela McAllister

Illustrated by
Margaret Chamberlain

Orion
Children's Books

First published in Great Britain in 2013 by Orion Children's Books
a division of the Orion Publishing Group Ltd
Orion House
5 Upper Saint Martin's Lane
London WC2H 9EA
An Hachette UK Company

3 5 7 9 10 8 6 4 2

The Orion Publishing Group's policy is to use papers that are
natural, renewable and recyclable products and made from wood
grown in sustainable forests. The logging and manufacturing
processes are expected to conform to the environmental
regulations of the country of origin.

A catalogue record for this book
is available from the British Library.

Printed and bound in China

www.orionbooks.co.uk

For Sophie, with thanks for all her help, and for everyone at the Fordingbridge Dance Studios.

Contents

Chapter 1   11

Chapter 2   23

Chapter 3   29

Chapter 4   39

Chapter 5   53

Chapter 6   63

Chapter One

This is Sophie.

She loves her mum and dad
and her baby brother, Max.

She loves anything that
sparkles.

And everything pink.

And she loves to dance!

Sometimes Sophie dresses up as a princess and dances around the house.

Sometimes she pretends to be a fairy and dances around the garden.

'I wish I was a proper dancer in a show,' said Sophie. 'At the end of a show a proper dancer curtseys and all the people clap.'

Sophie decided to put on her own show.

She made tickets for her toys.

'Sit still now,' she told them, 'and don't talk.'

Sophie
danced a jiggy,
jumpy dance,

then a
swooping,
swaying
dance,

then she hopped and skipped
and waved her arms high.

The toys sat very, very still and didn't talk.

But at the end, when Sophie curtseyed, nobody clapped. Max just sucked his thumb happily.

'Oh dear, it's not a real show without clapping,' said Sophie sadly.

She didn't feel like a proper dancer at all.

Chapter Two

On Sophie's birthday, two presents were waiting for her at the breakfast table.

The first present was a
sparkling pink bag.

'I love it,' said Sophie.
'Thank you. I'm going to take it
everywhere!'

The second present was a
ballet book with lots of pictures.
Sophie's favourite was a picture
of a beautiful dancer with
flowers in her hair.

That afternoon Grandma came to tea. She gave Sophie a present tied with a pink ribbon. It was a glittering wand.

Mum tied the pink ribbon in
Sophie's hair and Sophie danced
for Grandma.

As Sophie danced she wished that one day she would be a proper dancer, just like the ballerinas in her book.

Chapter Three

Next morning Mum and Sophie went shopping.

'What are we going to buy?' she asked.

'You are old enough to have ballet lessons now, so we are off to buy the things you'll need,' said Mum.

Mum took Sophie to the
ballet shop.

She gave the lady behind
the counter a list of things that
Sophie would need.

1 pink leotard
1 pair pink tights
1 pink chiffon skirt
1 pink cardigan
Ballet shoes

The shop lady found
everything on the list and Sophie
tried them on.

Sophie looked at herself in the
shop mirror and pointed her toes,
just like the dancer in her book.

The clothes were too special
to wear outside, so the shop lady
packed them all up carefully and
gave them to Sophie.

Sophie put the shoes in her
bag and carried them home
proudly.

That night, Sophie laid her
ballet clothes on a chair beside
her bed.

The moon shone between
the curtains and sparkled on
her wand.

Sophie yawned. She couldn't wait for her first ballet lesson. Maybe she really would be a proper dancer one day.

Chapter Four

On the day of the ballet class
Sophie woke up early and danced
around her room in her nightie.

Max started to cry so Sophie
went to see him.

'Poor Max,' said Sophie.
'He'll cheer up when we go
into town,' said Mum.

Sophie felt excited and nervous. She picked up her wand. It will help me to feel brave, she thought.

When they arrived, the ballet school was very busy. Sophie held her wand tight.

'Hello, Sophie,' said Miss Lucy, the teacher. 'Welcome to our class.'

Miss Lucy showed Sophie where to change her shoes and introduced her to the other girls.

Then they all lined up and
Miss Lucy led them into the
dance studio.

A man sat at the piano,
ready to play the music.

First, the girls sat on the floor
and Miss Lucy called the register.

Then she told them to stand
in a circle and pretend to be
beautiful birds.

'Skip lightly and stretch your
wings,' said Miss Lucy.

Next Sophie had to be a rocket
ready for take off. Three, two, one,
lift off! She bounced and jumped
as high as she could.

Then the girls sat on the floor and pretended to ride a bicycle, stretching their legs and pointing their toes. Sophie tried not to giggle.

'Now I want everyone to reach up and pick stars gently out of the sky,' said Miss Lucy.

Sophie imagined a starry sky above them.

'I think we are all warmed up,' said Miss Lucy, 'so we are ready to learn First Position.'

Chapter Five

'The first thing every ballerina learns is First Position,' said Miss Lucy.

The girls watched carefully.

'Heels are kissing,' said Miss Lucy, 'but bad toes have had an argument and don't want to look at each other.'

Sophie watched and copied
what Miss Lucy did.

She stood up straight and looked in the big mirror – at last she was learning to be a proper dancer!

Sophie learned how to half-
bend by making a diamond
window with her legs.

She learned how to point, and tap her foot gently, as if she was a princess wearing a glass slipper.

Then she learned how to trot
like a pony.

Sophie loved it all.

When it was time to finish,
Miss Lucy showed everyone how
to curtsey with their feet in first
position.

'Well done, girls,' she said.
'You danced beautifully.'

Sophie noticed a poster
of a dance show on the wall.

I'm going to be a proper
dancer in a show just like that
one day, she thought.

Sophie wanted to rush out to tell Mum everything, but she had to walk nicely in line, just like a proper dancer.

Chapter Six

Mum was waiting with all the other mums and dads and brothers and sisters.

'Did you enjoy the class?' she asked.

'Oh, yes!' said Sophie, giving her a hug. 'We even did a curtsey at the end. Look, Max...'

Max looked at his sister, but
his eyes scrunched up. He started
to cry again.

'Oh dear,' said Mum. Max
cried so loudly that the other
children began to cry too.

'That baby's got a tooth coming,' said one of the mums.

'Poor Max,' said Mum. 'I think you're right.'

Sophie had an idea. She began
to dance.

As soon as Sophie started to dance, Max stopped crying. All the children stopped crying.

Sophie
fluttered like
a bird.

She jumped
like a shooting
rocket.

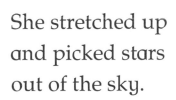

She stretched up
and picked stars
out of the sky.

Last of all, she pointed her
pink, satin toes and imagined she
was the beautiful dancer from
her book.

Then Sophie stood in First
Position and curtseyed.

All the mums and dads and
the girls and their brothers and
sisters clapped.

Max was smiling and laughing too.

'That was a lovely show, Sophie,' said Miss Lucy.

Sophie beamed.

It had been a real show, with real ballet shoes and a curtsey and clapping at the end!

At last she felt like a proper dancer.

What are you going to read next?

More adventures with

or go to
sea with

Horrid Henry,

or into space with

Poppy the Pirate Dog,

You could
have fun
on

Cudweed.

A Rainbow Shopping Day,

or explore

Down in the Jungle,

but watch out for

A Creepy Crawly Story!

Make magic with

The Three Little Witches,

and have
a ball
with

Princesses.

Or follow the star in

The First Christmas.

Enjoy all the Early Readers.

Sign up for **the orion star** newsletter
for all the latest children's book news,
plus activity sheets, exclusive competitions,
author interviews, pre-publication extracts
and more.

www.orionbooks.co.uk/newsletters

Follow @the_orionstar on **twitter**.

Orion
Children's Books